How to Travel
with Grownups

Elizabeth Bridgman

How to Travel
with Grownups

Pictures by Eleanor Hazard

Thomas Y. Crowell   New York

To Zachary, Nathan, and Ben

Library of Congress Cataloging in Publication Data

Bridgman, Elizabeth P.
  How to travel with grownups.
  SUMMARY: Offers helpful hints to youthful wayfarers
who travel with grownups.
  [1. Travel—Fiction] I. Hazard, Eleanor Lanahan.
II. Title.
PZ7.B7624Ho   [E]   79-2775
ISBN 0-690-04009-1   ISBN 0-690-04010-5 lib. bdg.

1 2 3 4 5 6 7 8 9 10

First Edition

How to Travel
with Grownups

Leave the big bears at home,

also the guinea pigs.

It takes a long time to get there,

so take a little knapsack full of things,

but don't spill it.

Stay with your parents.

Rest occasionally.

Don't kick the back of the seat.

No paper airplanes here,

and no ketchup.

Try not to set a bad example for the younger children.

Don't horse around the fountains,

and don't lose your shoe.

Always obey the captain.

Don't stare at strangers.

Pay attention to your ice cream.

Don't get hurt.

Sometimes sleep late,

and go to the bathroom whenever you can.

Be very polite to customs officers.

Be extra quiet here.

Wear some identification.

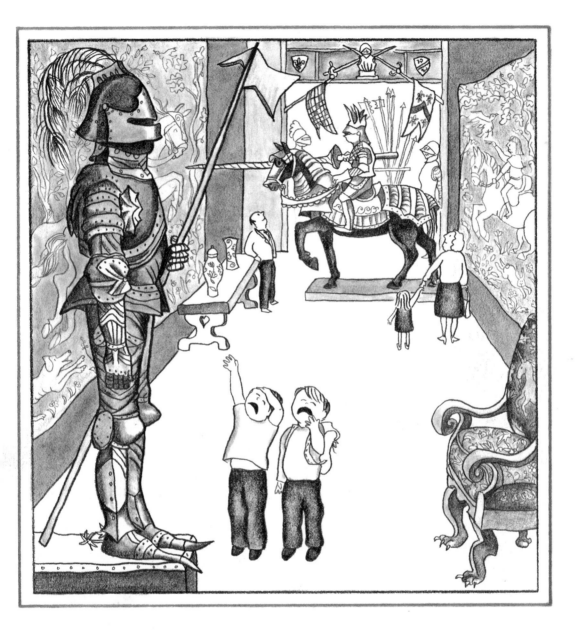

If you do get lost, tell a person in uniform,

but most of all, have a good time!